D1455364

Sir William the Worm

Written by Gary Hogg

Illustrated by Gary R. Anderson

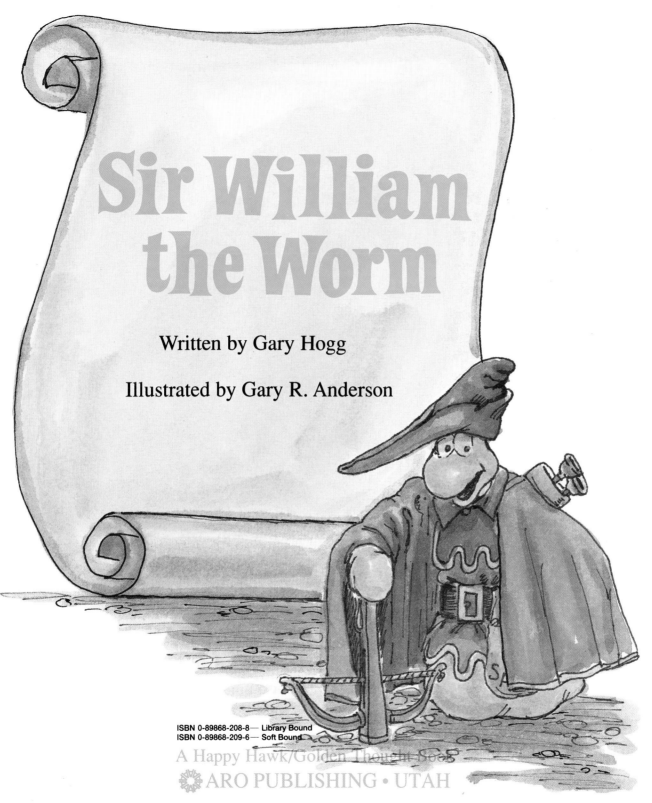

ISBN 0-89868-208-8 — Library Bound
ISBN 0-89868-209-6 — Soft Bound

A Happy Hawk/Golden Thought Book

ARO PUBLISHING • UTAH

Deep in the underneath, below the moon and the stars,
Below cities and towns with their beep-beep cars,
Below cats chasing mice and dogs scratching fleas,
Below the chirp of birds and the buzz of bees,
Below bugs and spiders that make people squirm,
Lies the mystical, magical world of the worms.

Worms don't drive cars, and they can't ride bikes.
They don't like to jog, and they really hate hikes.

They travel through tunnels,

through in-and-out holes.

They avoid the gophers.

They make way for the moles.

Wiggle worms are young. They're just starting out.
They giggle and wiggle and squirm all about.
Angle worms are thinkers. They plan and devise.
When it comes to worm matters, they are always wise.

Knight Crawlers are the most
noble worms of all.
They stand for truth and right
wherever they crawl.
In order for a worm
to become a Knight,
He must prove he is brave,
honest and right.

6

William was a wiggler with a very big dream.
He wanted to be part of the Knight Crawler team.

He had to prove he wasn't afraid of bird or man.
So William thought up a very dangerous plan.
He was sure that his plan would make the worms gawk.
He would crawl to the surface and capture a hawk.

When William popped his head out of the ground,
He squinted his eyes and began looking around.
Suddenly, without warning and to William's surprise,
The Happy Hawk landed right before his eyes.

His heart began to pound, and his head grew light.
Here was his chance to prove he could be a Knight.
He went right to work. He wasted no time.
He crawled to the Hawk's leg and began to climb.

Up the Happy Hawk's leg
William did race.
Up, up, until he reached
the Hawk's face.

He climbed up the beak and looked the Hawk in the eye.
He yelled, "Surrender, bird brain, or you will die.
Come with me; there is not a thing you can do.
I'm William, the Worm, and I've captured you!"

"Hmmm," said the Hawk.

"You've got me fair and square.
But I'd like to take one

last flight in the air."

And before William could say
even one more word,
He was flying high in the sky
on the beak of the bird.
"Put me down," said William.
"I'm afraid of heights.
Put me down and there won't
be any more fights."

14

"Sorry," said the Happy Hawk, "but we're not through.

Perhaps you have bitten off more than you can chew."

Higher and higher the Happy Hawk did soar.
"Stop," yelled William. "I can't take any more.
Please, oh, please end this scary flight.
I just did it so I could become a Knight."

The Happy Hawk then turned his flight around.
Soon he set William safely on the ground.

"William the Worm, before I send you on your way,
There are a couple of things I want to say.
There's nothing wrong with wanting to be a Knight.
But you should think twice before you pick a fight.

You are a brave little worm, it's clear to see.
But don't use your courage to try to hurt me.
Helping, not hurting is what a Knight would do."
He gave William a feather, and off he flew.

William learned something from the Hawk that day.
Courage should only be used in a kind, helpful way.
He took the feather and went back down in the ground.
When he got home he heard a loud, cheering sound.

The worms saw the feather and they thought of a fight.
"Hooray," they yelled. "William can become a Knight!"

"I'm sorry," said William. "I can't be a Knight.
The way I used my courage just wasn't right.
Someday I'll use my courage to do something good.
I'll help someone in need like a real Knight would."

The King of all the worms then raised his voice.
"I've seen what you've done, and I've made my choice.
You could have fooled us but told the truth instead.
You have the right kind of courage," the King Worm said.

"For your courage and honesty, it is only right
That I dub you Sir William, the Royal Knight."